"For my sweetest Eliza Mae."

ONE NICE THING

By Madeline Farrar

Illustrated by Vidya Lalgudi Jaishankar

One bright and shining morning,
Eliza had an idea.

She jumped out of bed and got ready for school
to tell her best friend Mia!

4

She said, "Mia, you make me smile,
And with that I propose,
You say one nice thing to the next person you meet,
And we'll see how far this goes!"

"Sounds great!" replied Mia. As she marched right down the hall,
She came across Zoey wearing a pink-and-green-striped shawl.

"Zoey, you have got style,
And with that I propose,
You say one nice thing to the next person you meet,
And we'll see how far this goes!"

Zoey smiled ear-to-ear, feeling better than before.
She then found Zariah, prancing through the gymnasium doors.

Grade 02

SPORTS
DAY !

"Zariah, I admire you,
And with that I propose,
You say one nice thing to the next person you meet,
And we'll see how far this goes!"

Zariah loves Nora's dance moves.

Nora thinks Hazel is a hoot!

Hazel sat next to Charlotte on the bus and exclaimed, "You are so cute!"

Now Eliza is proud of her friends,
As she sees the deed is done.

She will start again tomorrow, because being nice is
OH SO FUN!

One (More) Nice Thing

Here are more ideas of nice things to say to one another.

If you have your own ideas, write them on the following page!

You are a very hard worker.

Your hair is lovely.

You light up the room.

Your smile makes me smile.

You always share with me.

You are so strong.

Thank you for being my friend.

I am so proud of you.

I like your nails.

You are doing a great job.

You are smart.

You make me happy.

I like your ideas.

One (More) Nice Thing : Activity Page

Grab a pen/pencil! Fill out the blanks below with

your own ideas of nice things to say to one another:

_____

_____

_____

_____

_____

_____

_____

_____

_____

CPSIA information can be obtained
at www.ICGtesting.com
Printed in the USA
LVHW061439060323
741034LV00008B/700